S0-DRH-151

# Beach Bird

## Carol and Donald Carrick

The Dial Press • New York

Copyright © 1973 by Carol and Donald Carrick
All rights reserved. Library of Congress Catalog Card Number 72-703
Printed in the United States of America
First Pied Piper Printing
A Pied Piper Book is a registered trademark of The Dial Press.

BEACH BIRD is published in a hardcover edition by
The Dial Press, 1 Dag Hammarskjold Plaza, New York, New York 10017.
ISBN 0-8037-0416-X

To Jane Damroth

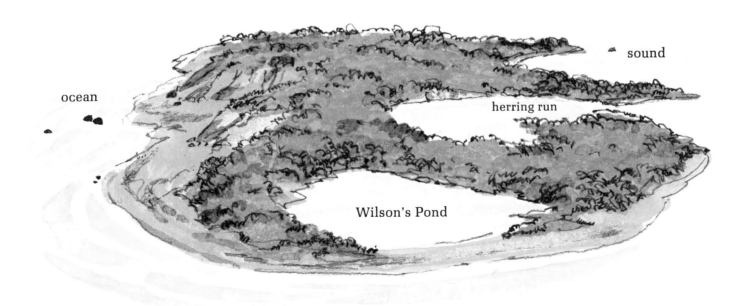

ocean

sound

herring run

Wilson's Pond

Just after dawn the geese rose from Wilson's Pond. Their honks and splashes woke the seagull, who had floated all night on the quiet water.

The gull flew over the dunes toward the ocean. Sand drifted inland, pushed by the shoulder of the wind. It was held back by the beach grass, roots driving deep in search of water, leaves reaching above the blowing sand.

The sun rose higher in the sky. A wolf spider crept to the shade of a beach plum, away from the searing heat that could dry up his blood.

Row after row of waves raced one another to shore. The seagull floated up one side of a wave, disappeared behind it, and floated up the side of the next.

As the tide went out, it had left quiet pools protected by rocks from the hammering waves. The rocks were overgrown with seaweed like mermaids' hair and hung with chains of shiny mussels.

A starfish crept out from its cave. It struggled to force apart a mussel's shell and eat its tender body.

The gull flew along the valleys of the waves, watching the sandy bottom. He dropped to the water, ducked his head under, and rose with a moon snail in his beak.

He circled high over the beach and dropped the hard shell to shatter it on the rocks below. But swooping down to grab his prize, he lost it among the other broken shells and stones.

The hungry bird joined another gull perched on a rock. They let small waves wash over their feet. When larger ones broke, they flapped above the spray and settled back again.

The two birds carefully examined the seaweed. As the tide came back in, periwinkles began to slide over the rock, scraping off the plants with their toothy tongues. But before the snails had finished their meal, they were eaten themselves by the gulls.

The gull washed his beak and with it preened the feathers that kept him waterproof. He flew across the island toward the sound, passing over swallows nesting in the cliffs.

The night before, horseshoe crabs had crawled out of the sound to lay their eggs. One, too slow to leave with the tide, was still on shore. The gull swooped down to flip her over and eat her soft underside. But digging with a sharp shell and strong legs, she soon bulldozed safely under the sand.

High above the beach, a mother osprey sailed in wide circles, looking for fish. Back in her nest, open mouths were screeching.

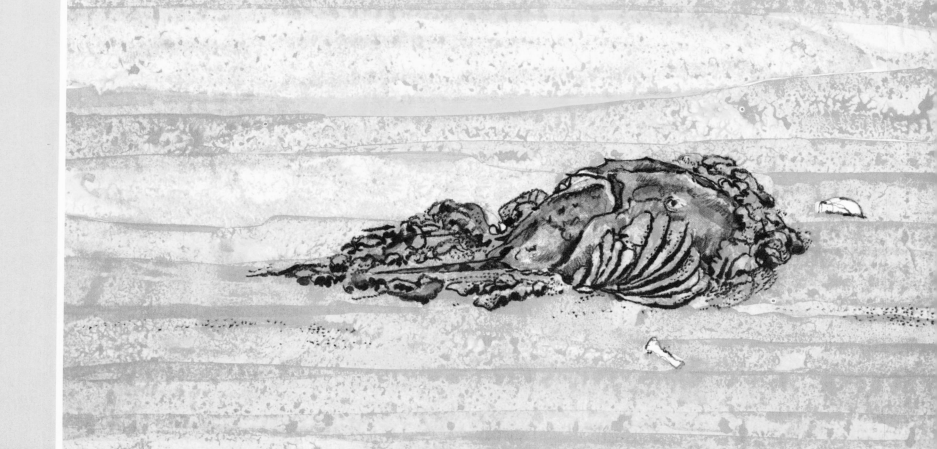

The gull saw a spider shape moving along the muddy bottom. He dropped to the water, struck with his beak, and came up dangling a crab.

Carrying his struggling catch to the beach, he stabbed open its shell. But a few feet away, he saw the remains of another gull's meal. While he greedily went to investigate, his own half-eaten crab headed back to the water. Seeing his mistake, the gull finished the dinner he had almost lost, leaving only ten crab legs that were now still.

The channel that ran from Herring Pond to the sound was speckled with gulls. The herring had laid their eggs in the pond and were returning to the sea. As the fish crowded through the shallow waterway, they made an easy target.

Excited by the cries of the others, the gull swept down through the squabbling birds. He spent the rest of the afternoon at the herring run gobbling fish, stealing scraps, and dropping his own beakful to scream warnings at gulls who came too close.

Finally, he could eat no more. He flew steadily toward the peace of Wilson's Pond.

The geese had also returned for the night. They bobbed gently, now and then dipping their dark heads to pull up dripping water plants. A pair of swans, about to take their hatchlings for a paddle, hissed at him as he landed. Weary of confusion and battle, the gull left.

Sandpipers were running up the beach ahead of the incoming waves. As the water washed back into the ocean, they poked into the wet sand for mole crabs. Along the high water mark, other birds turned over shells and bits of wood and searched through dry seaweed.

Fog moved in. Daylight and the hunting birds left the shore.

Safe for the night, shellfish half-buried in the shallows pumped water in and out, sifting food from the surf. Beach fleas began to clean up dead fish and bits of sea lettuce.

The gull's fierce bill was hidden in his snow-white feathers. He slept standing, by the edge of the sea.

Carol and Donald Carrick have collaborated on several children's books on nature themes, including A CLEARING IN THE FOREST and THE BLUE LOBSTER (both Dial).

Carol Carrick was born in New York and was graduated from Hofstra University. She has worked as an art director for an advertising firm, but now devotes her time to writing.

Donald Carrick was born and raised in Dearborn, Michigan. He studied art at Colorado Springs Fine Arts Center and at the Vienna Academy of Art in Austria. After traveling and painting in Europe, he settled in New York, where he has had several one-man shows.

For many years Carol and Donald Carrick have spent a few days each year at Martha's Vineyard, the setting for BEACH BIRD. But it wasn't until they went back to research the book that they decided to move there permanently. They now live with their two sons in Beach Bird's sun-dazzled, fog-shrouded home on Martha's Vineyard.